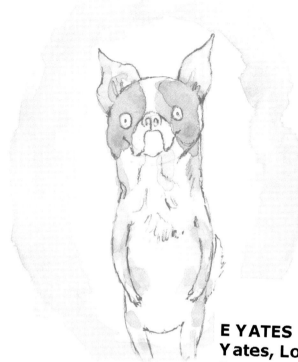

Date: 1/23/12

E YATES
Yates, Louise.
Dog loves books /

DOG LOVES BOOKS

LOUISE YATES

Alfred A. Knopf
New York

Dog loved
books.

He loved
the smell
of them,

and he loved the feel of them.

He loved everything about them....

Dog loved books so much

that he decided to open
his own bookstore.

He unwrapped,

unpacked,

and stacked
the books,
ready for the
Grand Opening.

When the day of the
Grand Opening
finally came,
Dog had a bath,

dried his fur,

blew his nose,

and threw open the door

to greet his new customers.

But there was no one there.

So Dog tried to keep busy.

And then . . .

a lady came into the store.

"I'll have a tea with milk and two sugars,"
she said.

"I'm sorry," said Dog, "but this is a bookstore. I only sell books."

The lady walked out.

Dog
was
alone.

He
waited
and
waited.

Then a man came into the store . . .

to ask for directions.

When he left, Dog was downhearted.

But not for long!

He wouldn't wait a
moment more.

Dog fetched a book from the shelf
and began to read.

When he read,
he forgot
that he was
waiting.

When he read,
he forgot that
he was alone.

When he read,
he forgot that
he was in the
bookstore.

And when one adventure ended, Dog simply took another book down from the shelf and . . .

a new
adventure began!

So Dog was somewhere else altogether when . . .

a customer came into the store to ask
for a book.

Dog knew
exactly
which
ones to
recommend.

Dog loves books

but most of all . . .

he loves to share them!

For Eleanor and Cedric

THIS IS A BORZOI BOOK PUBLISHED BY ALFRED A. KNOPF

Copyright © 2010 by Louise Yates

All rights reserved. Published in the United States by Alfred A. Knopf, an imprint of Random House Children's Books, a division of Random House, Inc., New York.
Originally published in 2010 in Great Britain by Jonathan Cape, an imprint of Random House Children's Books.
Knopf, Borzoi Books, and the colophon are registered trademarks of Random House, Inc.

Visit us on the Web! www.randomhouse.com/kids

Educators and librarians, for a variety of teaching tools, visit us at www.randomhouse.com/teachers

Library of Congress Cataloging-in-Publication Data
Yates, Louise.
Dog loves books / Louise Yates. — 1st American ed.
p.   cm.
Originally published: Great Britain : Jonathan Cape, 2010.
Summary: Dog loves books so much that he decides to open a book store.
ISBN 978-0-375-86449-0 (trade) — ISBN 978-0-375-96449-7 (lib. bdg.)
[1. Dogs—Fiction. 2. Books and reading—Fiction.] I. Title.
PZ7.Y276Do 2010
[E]—dc22
2009011097

The illustrations in this book were created using pencil and watercolor.

MANUFACTURED IN MALAYSIA
September 2010
10 9 8 7 6 5 4 3
First American Edition

Random House Children's Books supports the First Amendment and celebrates the right to read.